A is for **adorable**, which describes Lyra each and every day.

B is for **brave**. Lyra doesn't let fear get in the way!

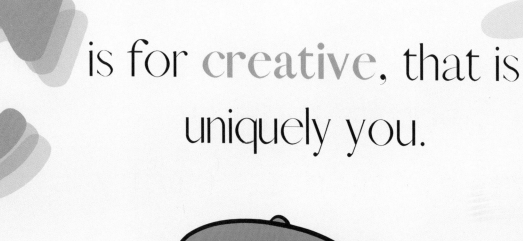 is for **creative**, that is uniquely you.

is for **dreamer**,
that keeps Lyra
true!

is for **eager** to learn new things each day!

F is for **fantastic**. Which describes Lyra in every way!

G is for giving, that is a kind thing to do.

H

is for Lyra hugs, that
keep others from
feeling blue.

I is for imagination, pretending is best!

J is for joy, that Lyra brings to all the rest!

K is for **kindness** the greatest way to be!

L is for laughter. Sweet special giggles for Lyra and me.

M is for magical. A fun way to play!

N is for noble. The way
we all strive to stay.

O is for one-of-a-kind.
That is definitely you!

P is for **priceless** which Lyra is that too!

Q is for quirky, so silly and fun!

R is for **remarkable**. Lyra is remarkable from moon until sun!

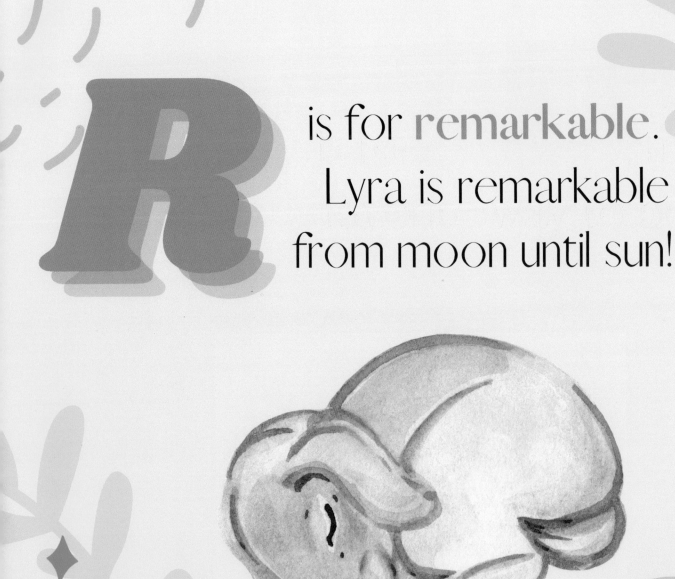

S is for special, like you are to me.

T is for together, my favorite way to be.

U is for **unique**, Lyra that has always been you!

V is for **vibrant**, the way your heart shines so true.

W

is for wonder,
while I watch you
grow.

X is for e**X**cited, to see what you know.

Y is for YOU, to know exactly who <u>you</u> are.

Z is for zig zags, I take for you whether near or far.

Lyra I love
you from
A - Z
Love,

_____

Printed in Great Britain
by Amazon

36218987R00016